A MAGIC CIRCLE BOOK

The Little Elephant Who Liked to Play

by **NAOMI SELLERS**
illustrated by **YOKO MITSUHASHI**

THEODORE CLYMER
SENIOR AUTHOR, READING 360

GINN AND COMPANY
A XEROX EDUCATION COMPANY

Home Office, Lexington, Massachusetts 02173
Library of Congress Catalog Card Number: 73-77986
0-663-25473-6

Little Elephant wanted to be a good little elephant. He wanted to do all the things his mother asked him to do. But he liked to play too.

One day all the elephants were going far away to look for a new home. Mother Elephant said to Little Elephant, "I want you to eat a good meal and take a nap to get ready for the trip."

Little Elephant said, "Yes, Mother."

But he didn't want to eat, and he didn't want to sleep. He wanted to play.

Little Elephant kicked a log across the grass. Then he saw a line of ants and followed them to the river. There he saw Little Deer.

"Look," said Little Elephant, "I'm a duck!" And he jumped into the river. Little Elephant wanted to swim and play. "Quack, quack," he said.

Little Deer looked at him in surprise and said, "What a BIG duck you are!"

Then Little Deer said, "Little Elephant, I hear Mother Elephant calling you."

Little Elephant came up and looked at Little Deer. He had not finished playing yet. "Go and tell my mother that I can't come now," he said.

Little Deer looked down at Little Elephant deep in the river. "Are you in danger?" she asked.

"Yes," said Little Elephant.

"Then I will run and tell Mother Elephant," said Little Deer.

Little Deer ran to find Mother Elephant. She was eating the top leaf from a big tree.

"Come fast!" Little Deer said. "Come fast! Little Elephant can't get out of the river. He's in danger."

Mother Elephant looked at Little Deer and said, "Little Elephant can swim. Do you know that he's in danger?"

"Oh, yes," said Little Deer. "He said he was."

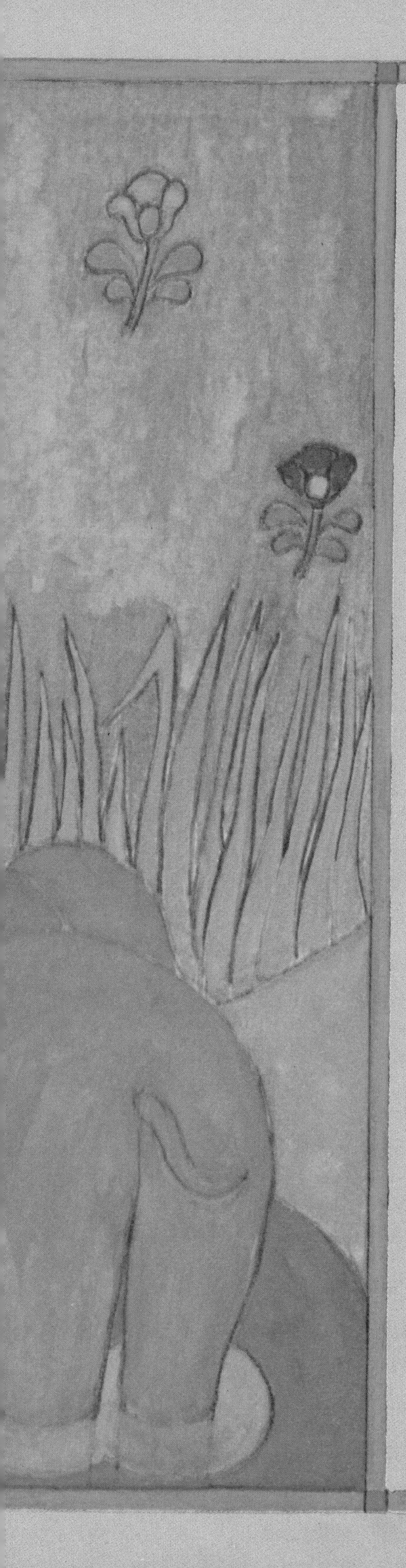

Mother Elephant asked the other elephants to wait for her. She ran from the trees to the river.

And there was Little Elephant still playing that he was a duck.

Mother Elephant called to Little Elephant, "Come out of there NOW!"

Little Elephant came out of the river fast. "I was just playing," he said.

"There is no time to play!" Mother Elephant said. "Go and eat. In a little while we are going far away to find a new home."

Little Elephant went to a little tree and ate a leaf. And Mother Elephant went up a hill to eat from the top of a big tree.

When Little Elephant looked up, he saw a red and green and yellow parrot. "A parrot sits in a tree with food all around him," Little Elephant said. "I will play that I'm a parrot."

Little Elephant sat down and then reached out to pick up the green grass all around him. It was fun playing that he was a parrot.

Little Lion ran up to Little Elephant and looked at him. He asked, "Why aren't you standing up? Are you ill?"

"Yes," said Little Elephant. "I can't get up. I can't walk."

"I will run and tell Mother Elephant," said Little Lion.

Little Lion ran across the grass and up the hill to Mother Elephant.

"Little Elephant is ill," he said. "He can't walk."

"Do you KNOW that he's ill?" asked Mother Elephant.

"Oh, yes," said Little Lion. "He said he was."

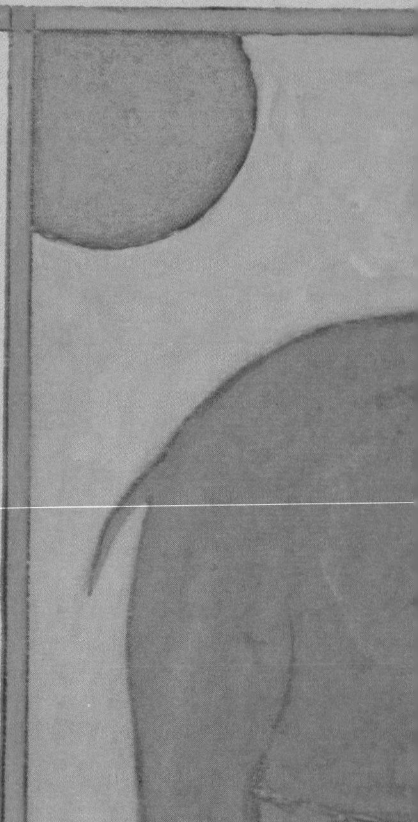

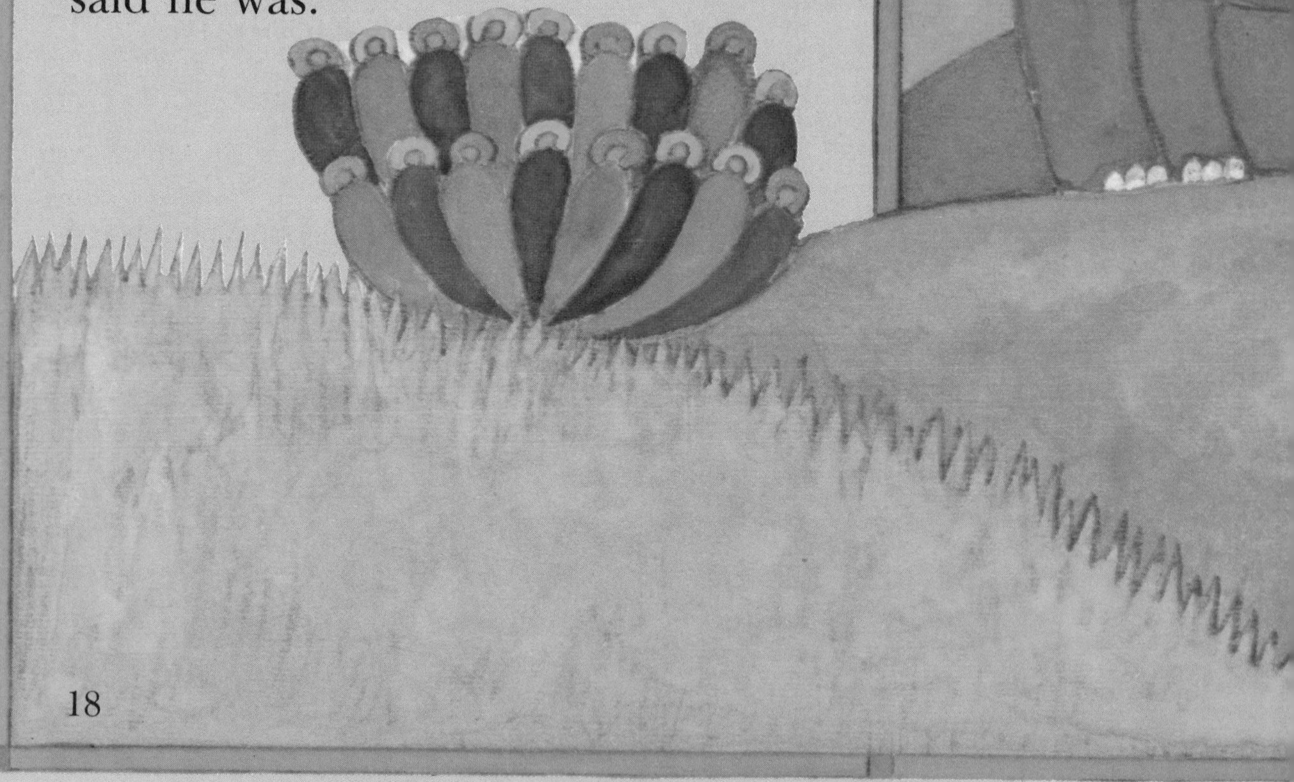

Mother Elephant went to Little Elephant. She picked up a big stick on the way.

"I will help you get up," she said to Little Elephant.

Little Elephant got up fast and ran to some trees.

Mother Elephant followed him. "This is no time to play! It's too late to eat now," she said. "It's time to go. Follow me."

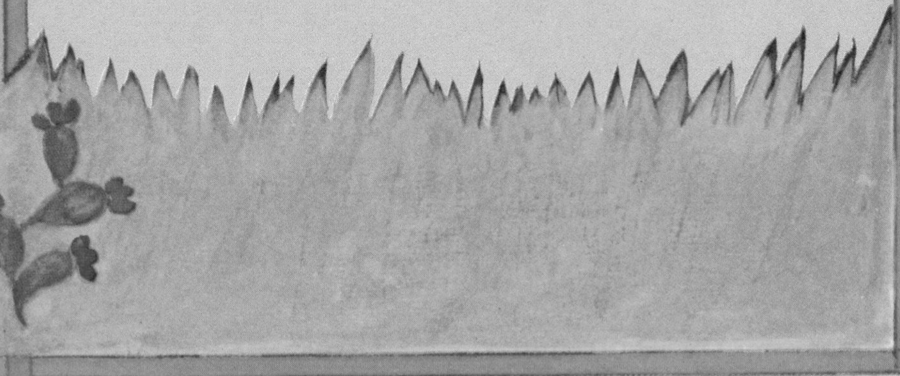

Little Elephant followed his mother and all the big elephants till he saw something new to play on. He walked up to it. It was fun to have something new to play on.

Little Elephant stopped in surprise when his foot got stuck. "Help! Help!" he called. "I can't walk!"

Little Ape ran across the grass. "Why are you here, Little Elephant?" she asked.

"I'm in a trap," said Little Elephant. "My foot is stuck! Go and tell my mother to come and help me. I'm in danger!"

"I hear something," said Little Ape.

Little Elephant looked up. He saw something big with a yellow eye. It hissed like a snake.

"Tell my mother a big snake is going to kill me," said Little Elephant. "Run fast!"

The big hissing thing came on and on.

Little Elephant called, "Help! Help!"

Little Ape saw the thing and ran across the grass to find Mother Elephant.

Then Little Elephant's mother came with all the big elephants. She stopped near Little Elephant. The big hissing thing stopped too.

All the elephants lined up near the hissing thing and looked at it. Its yellow eye looked back at them.

Mother Elephant went to Little Elephant and said, "If you shake your foot a little, you will be free."

Little Elephant did just what his mother asked him to do. When he was free, he ran away from the big hissing thing and hid in the trees.

Mother Elephant went to him and said, "Can you see that there is a time to play and a time not to play?"

"Yes, I can," said Little Elephant.

"Then do as I say," said Mother Elephant. "Follow me."

Little Elephant fell into line with his mother and all the big elephants.

When night came, Little Elephant looked up and saw a big yellow eye. "Look!" he said. "There's danger in the trees!"

Mother Elephant looked back at him. "What did you say?" she asked.

Little Elephant looked at his mother, and then he looked at the big yellow moon.

"I said that for a while—just for a little while—it looked like danger," Little Elephant said.

Mother Elephant walked on with the big elephants. Little Elephant followed for a little while.

Can you guess what Little Elephant did then?

CDEFGHIJK 765
PRINTED IN THE UNITED STATES OF AMERICA